WITCH CABIN

JAKE GALJOUR

Cover Design by Danielle Stamper

Full Moon Publishing, LLC
Glade Spring, VA
Fullmoonpublishingllc.com

ISBN: 1946232017
ISBN-13: 978-1946232014

CONTENTS

A NEW MOON

It was Halloween, October 31st, 1988, in an ominous, autumn forest of West Virginia at night. The moon was full and orange. The wind howled frightfully with a ghostly cry. There was a rural dirt road about 3 miles from the nearest highway. A car traveled down the crackling, thick fog road. Its bright lights blinded us as the large car passed on the desolate path. It was a police car; a 1986 Ford ltd Crown Victoria. The lights were brightly illuminated. The car was marked with Hampshire County Sheriff's Department on its side. The police car pulled down into a fog laden glade.

Through the thick blanket of mist, haunting the low-lying forest glade, there was an old log cabin. The cabin was very old, at least from the 1700s; a dark, evil presence emanated from it. The police car pulled in close to the cabin and parked. The sound of the door to the police cruiser opened and a cop stepped out. The officer observed his surroundings, hand on his service revolver half out of its holster. The gun, a Smith and Wesson model 10 was loaded with deadly .38 hollow points—ready to kill. The cop, who advanced to the front of his car, was tall and slim, and had light slicked back blonde hair. His badge on his chest shined from the glare of the moon. On his face he wore large silver patrol glasses. The officer's name was Billy Smith, a rugged 32-year-old deputy of the Hampshire County, West Virginia Sheriff's department. *Where are you?* he asks himself.

The door to the cabin slowly creaked open and the figure of a lady appeared. A woman walked out onto the porch of the cabin, and with a velvet voice she invited Officer Smith inside. The woman was young, in her mid 20s. She was beautiful with thick black hair. Her eyes were green and sultry, and her cheeks hued with deep blush. She was tall and her lips were a macabre deep blood red. On her curved smooth body, she wore only a silk black robe. The woman introduced herself as Teri Black.

Officer Smith was now inside…alone…standing in the bright blaze of the nearby fireplace. As the door closed behind them, he spoke, "Ms. Black, I am Deputy Billy Smith of the Hampshire County Sheriff's Department. I'm here to ask you a few questions regarding the homicide of your parents who were brutally murdered in the spring of '81… I believe you were 16 then." He asked her some questions and informed her that she was now a suspect due to some new evidence that had recently surfaced. He eventually found himself asking her if she enjoyed killing them the way she did.

Teri smiled, and in a shocking change of atmosphere and energy, unfastened her black silk night robe, revealing to him her large breasts. "Billy let's not live in the past. Make love to me," she demanded. Billy suddenly found himself frozen—no words, no thought, no control, and no more authority.

"God you're beautiful," he said. Teri grabbed him and pulled him in close to her causing their bodies to collide in the power of passion.

That night they had mind-bending, nerve-shattering sex in Teri's back bedroom of the old cabin. At dawn Teri slowly and quietly stood up and grabbed a large, rusty, double-bladed axe hidden under the mattress. Without warning she attacked and hacked the officer to a bloody, bone-crushing, gut-splashing, blood-spraying, violent, dismembering death. "Happy Halloween Billy," she laughed between gritted teeth. Teri, now blood soaked walked outside onto the porch to watch the morning mist come in.

ENTER THE WOODS

October 30th, 27 years later, in the bare autumn forest of northeast West Virginia the sun was setting. A mid-sized, silver BMW SUV drove on a major highway deep in the foothills of Hampshire County. Inside the SUV were a group of teenagers; their names where Paul, Jamie, Doug, Jim and Tina. They were all high school friends looking for their luxury cabin they had rented for Halloween. It was getting dark.

"I can't believe we put all our money together for a cabin we can't even find," said Jim, upset.

"Jim, we will find it, just relax," said Paul, the driver and oldest of the group.

"There sure is a lot of forest in this area," said Jamie, Paul's girlfriend.

"Eastern West Virginia has some of the most rugged foothills in America," said Doug.

"I think we're lost," Tina says.

Paul tried to console everyone by telling them they must be close.

"What's that up ahead?" asked Jamie, pointing to bright lights in the distance.

The teens were stopped by a sheriff's department roadblock on the highway. When they pulled up an officer walked up followed by two lesser deputies. The man was tall and had a large build to him, about 220 pounds. He had a thick dark mustache, and wore a beige sheriff's department uniform. He appeared to be in his mid - sixties.

"Happy Halloween guys. I'm Sheriff Ronald Thomas. What are you kids doing out here in a place like this tonight?" he asked.

Paul, the driver, answered him, "Sir, my friends and I have rented out a cabin for Halloween this year. It's not far from here. We were hoping to get there before dark, but it didn't work out the way we planned."

The sheriff asked them for the address and they gave it to him. Sheriff Thomas now gazed at the others in the SUV, cutting through them with his sharp grey-blue eyes. "Your cabin is about

11 miles up the highway; make sure you take the second right turn," he told them. Paul thanked him for his directions. The sheriff added a warning, "The past three decades, many young men have disappeared from this area, so when you get there…you make sure to lock the door at night."

A cold bone-chilling feeling gripped the friends after the sheriff's warning. Paul drove the SUV into the night and in the direction of the cabin.

The SUV pulled up a dirt road, off the highway. They couldn't agree on whether the sheriff had said the first or the second right turn. So they opted for the first right turn.

Paul said, "I hope we make it to the cabin; we are nearly out of gas."

A thick fog now rolled in, covering the area. "Paul, Paul pull over. We can't see; the fog is just too thick," pleaded Jamie as Paul began to think that he had taken the wrong turn.

Doug now looked on his smart phone "Paul, my signal has dropped, we're lost."

"Look out!" screamed Jamie, a large owl flew past the windshield causing a startled Paul to veer off the rural road and bottom out onto a nearby log. The SUV was immobilized.

"Is everyone ok?" asked Paul with concerned for his friends.

They all assured him they were fine.

"I can't believe that just happened" Paul said shocked.

"It's okay Paul, we're all okay," Jamie reassured him.

"Well, that's that. Everyone out," said Jim.

The teenagers reluctantly left the vehicle and look for help.

Through the fog a strange mist loomed over the road and strange noises radiated from the nearby fog thickened, skeleton trees of the forest. The friends navigated the long, mysterious road into the unknown. Paul was the leader of the group, and the oldest, was the star high school athlete back at the group's hometown. He was 18 years old with light blonde hair and sky-blue eyes. He was tall standing with a stout 190-pound build.

Jamie, Paul's girlfriend, walked next to him. She was a strong 17-year-old girl, and very even minded. Jamie was of medium stature, very fair complected with a red ponytail and soft, blue-green eyes.

Doug, the group's nerd, walked not far behind. He was the

tallest of the group, with deep blue eyes and brown hair and was thinly built. Always on his smart phone, the 17-year-old Doug was an aspiring writer: always conceiving a breakthrough horror or sci-fi story concept.

Jim was the group's bad boy. Jim was Italian born in New York City. He was smart mouthed and a frequent menace for the group's high school. He was almost 18 years old; he was tall slim but had a tough build to him. He wore a large blue denim jacket and tight blue jeans. He loved classic heavy metal music.

Finally, there was Tina. She was the attractive, but soft-spoken 17-year-old girlfriend to Jim, and also best friend to Jamie. She was dark, of French linage from Maine and had long dark, brown hair and warm brown eyes.

The group eventually came to the end of the rural dirt road where a huge, dead oak tree had fallen across the road

Jamie asked Paul how a tree of this size could have fallen over on the road, and never been moved.

"Maybe because no one has ever been out this deep into the woods before," Jim jumped in and responded.

"Look, a light!" exclaimed Jamie.

The group left the safety of the rural dirt road and followed the side path; deeper and deeper into the dead forest they followed the light. The fog became thicker, and the air became colder. The path now ascended into a low-lying glade in the woods.

"So Paul, what do you think that sheriff meant by disappearances the last 30 years?" Jamie asked.

"Do we really need to talk about that now?" yelled Tina, getting upset.

"Oh Tina, you're a little baby," cried Jim in a sarcastic response.

"Shut up Jim," snapped Jamie, getting upset at his attitude.

The group now emerged at an old cabin in a glade next to a grey, misty stream. The air was cold and the stream looked like ice. A sinking feeling now bore down on the group. The light that they had seen earlier had disappeared completely.

"This must be our cabin," declared Jim.

"It must be," said Jamie in agreement.

They walked up onto the old wood porch to the front door…sadly, however, the group had no idea the terror that awaited them.

WITCH CABIN

"Paul, you have tried unlocking the door ten times already. It won't work" said Jamie, bereaved of Paul's attempts on the door.

"Don't worry, I'll just kick in the door!" said Jim laughing.

A frustrated Tina exclaimed, "Are you crazy? This may not even be our cabin."

Jamie agreed. "Listen, even if it isn't, maybe someone living here may be able to help us find ours."

Paul interjected and reassured Jamie that it was their cabin. After a few more minutes of hesitation, Jamie suggests the possibility of a back door to the cabin. "Would any of you macho's like to walk around behind the cabin to check for a back door?" she asked. They all stand there in silence. "Alright then, I'll go," Jamie muttered as she walked off the porch and followed the log wall around the back corner of the cabin to what seems to be a large clearing with an axe standing in a tree stump. The area was blanketed in a thick cover of fog, and dead trees covered the area with the only sign of life being that of a horned owl in the distance perched on a tree. "I see you too," she said to the owl nervously. She looked over and to her amazement found a back door to the cabin. Strangely it was unlocked, so Jamie entered the cabin.

Jamie found herself in the kitchen of the cabin. "Oh my God," Jamie said to herself in amazement. Many lit candles lit the old, log kitchen, along with many Celtic and Druidic influenced charms and talismans along counters, walls and table. *What is this place?* she thought out loud. It was as if she found herself back in another time. Jamie now examined an old gas stove and coffee pot nearby. Jamie found a newspaper clipping on a small wood table, near a candle. *What's this?* she said to herself. The clipping showed two photos of a middle-aged man and woman and read:

March 24th, 1981. The gruesome murder of Mr. Stephen and Julia Bachmann cited by West Virginia law enforcers, including Deputy Sheriff Ron Thomas, as heinous crime—perhaps witchcraft involvement.

Jamie found herself in the living room. A blazing lit fireplace engulfed the room with a warm, living light, much better than the kitchen and warmer. Many antique trinkets and relics were displayed in the room including a six-foot oval mirror in the corner and a large clear crystal orb on a rosewood coffee table. Centering the room above the fireplace hung a large moose trophy; its eyes watched Jamie as she explored the room. She thought the whole place had an early 1700s feel to it. Jamie looked to the front door just beyond the fireplace. She walked over to unlock it. Jim jumped out from behind Jamie, scaring her terribly.

"You should have seen yourself! You looked like that owl outside!" he said.

"Shut the hell up Jim! That wasn't funny!" shouted Jamie angrily.

A strange unknown voice echoed from the dark from a nearby corner surprising them both. "She's right Jim, that wasn't funny." A woman appeared from the dark and walked up to them in the full light of the fire.

"Who are you?" asked Jamie.

"Who are you? What are you doing in my house?" asked the woman.

"I'm so, so sorry. We didn't know. My friends and I rented a cabin for Halloween. We got lost and thought this one was ours," Jamie remorsefully explained.

The woman smiled and told them in a relaxed tone that the rental cabin was about five miles west, closer to the highway.

"I knew we were off. Thank you for understanding," said Jim.

"It happens," said the woman. She then introduced herself, "My name is Teri, Teri Black. It's a pleasure." Teri invited the rest of the group waiting outside into her home for the evening.

DARK ACQUAINTANCES

In the living room around midnight Paul, Jamie, Jim, Doug and Tina sat around the warm crackling fireplace with their new charming yet mysterious friend, Teri Black. Teri was a very attractive woman; the mere sight of her excreted an overwhelming sexual desire for activity. The entire group was amazed with her conversation, as well as her overtaking sex appeal.

Teri was in her early fifties, yet her stunning appearance was at least ten years younger. Her defined look and fashion was that of mid-1980s Black Victorian or "Goth". Standing just under six feet without heels, she had a curved busted figure. She wore a black, very low cut dinner dress with a large plunging neckline, just barely short of revealing her massive breast. Teri's hair was full and raven black. She wore dark black eye shadow and crimson lipstick augmenting her thick seductive lips. Her piercing green eyes struck the group of teenagers, especially Jamie, with both curiosity and fear.

"So Teri, what exactly do you do?" asked Jim, clearly interested in getting to know the mysterious beauty. Teri responded, "Well, Jim, I'm a firm believer in the practice of Wicca. I believe everything…the trees, the water, even the air has a spirit. I firmly believe in karma, and what you do in this life will eventually come full circle. I'm a very spiritual person; I also cast spells and occasional rituals."

Everyone in the room glanced at one another, tongue tied and not sure what to say. Jim, clearly bewildered, finally spoke and told her that he was raised Roman Catholic but was never good at it.

The entire group, including Teri, erupted in laughter. "You guys are so funny. I wish I could keep you here with me," she said.

They all began to share stories about themselves and their likes with her; by the time they had finished, two full hours had passed.

"Ok guys, I don't know about you, but I'm ready to go to bed," said Paul, now clearly tired after a long, exhausting day.

"Same here," responded Tina, clearly ready to go to sleep after the long day.

Teri now told the group of friends that they are more than welcome to spend the night. "You can sleep in the living room, and stay for breakfast in the morning if you like," Teri said.

Paul told her that she was very sweet and they greatly appreciated the hospitality. The teenagers curled up on the cabin floor in front for the warm, crackling fire roaring in the large stone fireplace. Teri disappeared into a small, dark room toward the rear end of the cabin.

"Paul, I need to talk to you. I need to see you outside for a moment," said Jamie.

Paul followed Jamie out the front door and onto the porch in the moon's pale light where they began to talk. "Paul, do you trust this Teri woman? She seems pretty dark," she voiced her opinion.

"Jamie, right now Teri's the only person we have to trust. Can't you give her a chance? She only wants to help," he responded.

Jamie thought about what for Paul said for a moment and reluctantly agreed. "Yeah Paul, I guess you're right, maybe it's just me."

Paul assured Jamie that they would leave at daybreak and they walked back inside the cabin. Soon they fell asleep.

It was now 3:00 A.M. and Teri was still in her bedroom. The others were in a deep sleep. Teri sat on her old, small, wooden framed bed. Sitting there next to her on her wooden, antique nightstand was an old, discolored, torn photo of a young, red haired boy; the name "Daniel" inscribed under it. "I miss you," she said embracing the image. Teri stood up and put away the photo. She then began to light a large mass of candles lighting the small, wooden room with warm, bright light. Teri stooped down and reached under her bed, pulling out an antique Ouija board and laid it on her bed.

Teri began an old, Celtic chant begging it not to take a sacrifice for that year. Then, to her dissatisfaction, a message was spelled out on the board with the use of the planchette. KILL THEM.

Teri slowly arose and walked to the bedroom window and stared blankly into the predawn darkness. Then she began to plan the new season's harvest sacrifice.

AT THE CREEK

The next morning, October 31ˢᵗ, Paul, Jamie, Doug and Tina were cooking breakfast. The morning subject of conversation was none other than the various talismans and charms found throughout the room.

Doug made notice of the odd relics. "Teri sure does have a thing for the dark aspects of life," he commented.

Doug's comments agitated Paul, who was cooking. "Don't judge her Doug. Teri was kind enough to let us stay the night."

Tina, sitting at the table agreed. "That's right Doug; everyone has interests." Tina then asked Doug what was so interesting about his I-phone.

"It's a Galaxy, not an I-phone, and what's interesting is I still can't seem to get a signal. It's as if we dropped off the map when we arrived here," he told them.

Jim walked in the room. "Hey guys, where's the coffee?" he asked.

Paul poured him a cup.

"Hey guys, last night, when I came in the backdoor to the cabin, I found a newspaper article on the table here about some murders. It really creeped me out. It's not here this morning though."

"It was probably nothing important. Eggs are ready," Paul said and served the others.

Jim now peered out the nearby kitchen window; the morning was grey and a mist was coming in from the cold nearby stream. Soon Jim caught a glimpse of Teri, walking in the woods and he quickly excused himself. "Hey guys, I'm not very hungry so I'm going for a walk; I'll be back in a few minutes." Jim sat his coffee down and walked outside.

Paul shouted to him from behind, telling him they will be ready to leave soon, so to hurry.

"Since when is Jim fond of leisurely walks?" asked Paul.

Teri walked into the forest and downstream about one hundred feet from the cabin and walked up to a small sandbar. The morning was grey and cold and a ghostly mist hung hauntingly over the shallow stream. Teri was shrouded in mist, kneeled down over the bank and began what seemed to be a form of ritual. She began to chant.

Jim followed with some distance between them so he could observe her without her knowing. He hid behind a nearby dead tree and watched as Teri's true form of spiritual practice played out.

Teri ended her ritual, undressed and walked toward the stream.

What's this? What is she doing? Jim asked himself as he watched closely from the safety of the tree. Teri dipped her foot in the stream and entered the shallow stream. Jim peered hard to the sight of Teri, completely naked, and bathing in the stream. Teri rubbed a white liquid all over her body. From a distance Jim continued to watch in awe. Jim thought to *himself she must be a witch.*

As Jim watched from behind the tree, he noticed a marking on Teri's upper right arm, a marking, which he had seen before. It was a Rune; it was in the shape of a side-triangle and is known as the mark of Thorn. An icy wave of fear swept over Jim. Frightened, Jim stood up and ran away into the woods. A devilish smile swept over Teri's face as if she knew of the gazer all along… and who he was.

Jim quickly made his way back to the cabin but decided not to tell the others just yet. They were leaving soon anyway.

SEASONS CHANGE

At sunset the teens were forced to return to Teri's cabin after a long, unsuccessful day of searching for their cabin. There was no sign of Teri.

"We didn't even find the highway!" exclaimed a disappointed Doug.

They all walked up to Teri's front porch. Paul and Jamie told Jim, Doug and Tina to stay at the cabin for now. They were going to try to hike back to the rural road and get the SUV going. They also said that if they can get around the downed tree they would drive back to collect everyone at the cabin.

"Hopefully it will be before dark, and won't be long," said Paul. Then he and Jamie headed into the woods.

Tina, frustrated, exhausted and disappointed said to Jim, "This is insane! We should be at the rental cabin right now, watching horror films and eating popcorn. I wish we hadn't even come."

"It's okay Tina. Everything's okay. If Paul and Jamie aren't back in an hour, we'll walk up to the car to meet them. Just give them a chance," he said as he held her tightly.

After a few moments, Tina and Jim decided to go for a walk down to the creek.

Doug was alone on the cabins old, wooden front porch staring at his smart phone that had died earlier that day. "Great, just great," he said to himself aloud. "Now even my phone has left me." He sat there, observing the glade that the cabin sat in. A thick fog was now starting to ascend from the nearby stream, and a full, orange moon was rising slowly in the night sky. An owl watched Doug as if awaiting his certain doom. Soon the area flooded with mist. The cabin's front door opened and closed behind Doug. A startled Doug jumped a bit.

Teri Black walked out and sat down next to Doug on the porch steps. "The moon sure is nice tonight, soon it will cover the whole forest with its divine glow; Halloween is truly here."

"Yeah," said Doug in an unoptimistic tone. Teri asked him if he was okay. Doug told her how he and his friends had planned to spend Halloween. "We weren't supposed to have Halloween like this," he told her.

A seemingly understanding Teri put her hand on Doug's knee. "Yes—yes you were, you just didn't know it," she told him. Teri asked Doug, "Don't you have a girlfriend?"

"No. I'm the biggest nerd in West Virginia. While everyone in my class was busy getting jobs and girlfriends, I was working on my next failure of a book idea. The only reason Paul and Jamie brought me was so I wouldn't be alone," he told her.

Teri smiled and kissed him on the cheek. "Doug, you're not a nerd. The moment I laid eyes on you I got an indescribable feeling. You have such an effect on me." Teri took Doug by the hand and led him into the cabin and into her bedroom.

"Why are we here?" asked Doug.

"I need you Doug. I need you tonight," she told him as she dropped her dress.

"You're so beautiful" he told her. Then, like any teenage guy, immediately began to unbuckle his jeans.

Teri then took Doug. Little did he know she needed him for a specific and dark reason. "Doug, you did it!" she yelled laughing in satisfaction, thus Teri quickly pulled a rusty dagger from under the edge of the mattress and with one quick slash cuts Doug's manhood off then stabbed him several times in the chest. Blood flooded the room, spilling and spraying over the wooden walls, turning the room red with live blood. Doug franticly thrashed around the room before he fell to the floor dead.

OLD WOUNDS

On the secluded dirt road, about half a mile from the old cabin, Paul and Jamie had found their SUV. They spent two hours attempting to unearth its side left wheels from the ditch where it had bottomed out the day before. Jamie sat in the driver's seat and gave it gas as Paul attempted to pick up on that side. Sadly, Paul wasn't strong enough.

"Jamie, I don't think we'll ever get it out," he told her, sadness in his voice.

Jamie got out and told Paul they didn't have too; that they can walk the dirt road back to the highway and get help.

"It's a good two-mile walk…but we can try it," he told her. They began their long walk. Then suddenly, an array of bright lights arose from the foggy darkness gliding toward Paul and Jamie.

"Who could it be?" asked Jamie as the lights came closer. Then the lights came to a stop.

Paul and Jamie heard a familiar voice echo from behind the lights, "Are you kids okay? We have been looking for you."

In great relief Jamie and Paul ran toward the familiar voice of Sheriff Ronald Thomas, the policeman from the highway the night before. Without hesitation they got into the police car.

"Officer, we are so glad to see you! Our car bottomed out the other night and we have been stranded," Jamie told the Sheriff.

"I've been on the search for you and your friends all night. The owner of the rental cabin was concerned when you didn't show up. He told the sheriff's department that you never arrived," replied the sheriff.

Paul told the sheriff that they ended up at the wrong cabin and the owner, Teri Black, invited them to stay the night and how they had tried to find their cabin but couldn't and that the others were still at Teri's cabin waiting on them to find help.

The sheriff became uneasy with Paul's statement. "Teri Black…eh?" the sheriff replied and then became silent.

After a moment Jamie broke the silence and asked the sheriff what was wrong. He glanced in his rear view mirror, pale and with an expression of dread. The quick blink of his eyes showed them the fear and concern inside his soul.

He began to tell Jamie and Paul what occurred in the past. "Back in the mid 1980s we started receiving reports of missing male teenagers in this area. Then rumors began to spread of Witchcraft. It was believed that a girl by the name of Karen Bachmann was involved in human sacrifices," he told them. "I was familiar with Karen since 1981, when I covered a murder case— the murder of her parent's. Even though we couldn't prove it I was convinced that she was guilty. Karen disappeared soon after. In 1988, years after the disappearances began, a star Deputy of mine, Billy Smith, stumbled across Karen. Soon after that Billy disappeared and we found him dead and dismembered in a rural pond. We were certain that Karen was responsible for his death as well, we couldn't prove it. I believe that Teri Black is actually Karen," the sheriff finished.

Jamie remembered the old news clipping she had found the previous evening and realized that the sheriff was correct in his assumption—Karen Bachmann was indeed Teri Black.

Just as Sheriff Thomas started to call dispatch for backup, a deer leapt out in front of the police car. The sheriff swerved to miss the deer and crashed his Crown Victoria police cruiser into a roadside birch tree. A few hours passed and Jamie began to rouse. She awoke to the moonlight shinning in her face. She saw that Paul was also beginning to regain consciousness; however, it was obvious that the sheriff was dead.

My head—it hurts, she said to herself aloud.

As Paul began to open his eyes Jamie began to shake him and plead with him to get up. "Get up. We have to escape this patrol car," she demanded.

It didn't take long before Paul was completely conscious—he noticed that his arm was hurting. He was shocked to see that it appeared to be broken in two places. "My arm Jamie, my arm. It hurts so bad," he said.

Still frantic, Jamie began to kick at the already broken back window until she was able to kick out the glass. The two squeezed out carefully—Jamie first then Paul with her help.

"We have to get back and warn the others!" exclaimed Paul.

"No Paul we need to find help and get you to a hospital. Then we'll call the police department to let them know what happened,"

Jamie demanded.

Paul refused, "You will get me into an ambulance or car and then you will go back for the group; I'm not going to let you go up there alone. Besides, I'm your boyfriend and you need me to protect you, remember?"

Jamie forced a smile, "Okay, let's go." Jamie and Paul now ran back into the forest, toward the cabin in the woods.

THE NEW HARVEST

As Tina and Jim were walking by the creek a dense fog rolled in causing them to lose one another. Tina was still walking by the creek the fog had lifted enough to let the full moon shine down on her. Tina, frantically calling out to Jim only received the response of her own eerie echo. She felt as though she were being watched. The only thing she saw was a strange owl perched in a nearby tree watching her.

Distraught, Tina sat down from exhaustion. What she wouldn't give for a warm bath to soothe her cold aching body. She heard footsteps in the distance, and noticed a shadow looming in the darkness. She called out, "Jim! Is that you? Jim, are you out there?" she asked, a feeling of cold dread looming over her. Suddenly she saw a figure jump into the water with a huge splash.

"I'm sorry! I'm sorry. I just had to do it though," Jim told her, laughing outrageously.

Tina furiously slapped him across the face. "Who the hell do you think you are? Where did you come from? Psychos-R-Us!" she screamed angrily.

Jim now apologized. But Tina wasn't accepting his apology. She stormed off. "Hey, where you going?" he asked.

"Away from you!" she responded and disappeared into the darkness.

Jim sulked as he sat down on a rock next to the creek alone. The fog became heavy once again. A cold feeling griped his stomach as he heard the snapping of nearby twigs. "Tina, is that you?" he asked, but no answer came. He looked around. "Listen, if you're going to get back at me, try harder okay." Jim now began to contemplate how he treated her and felt remorseful. As Jim stood he heard a noise erupt behind. He turned to find a figure standing next to him. It was Teri Black wielding a large, rusty steel, double-bladed axe in hand. "Where did you come from?" Jim asked taking a step back.

"You should really watch how you treat people Jim," Teri said, having heard his and Tina's earlier incident.

"Nice night for a walk, right?" Jim sarcastically asked.

"Nice night to die," she now replied.

Jim now walked up to Teri, getting in her face. "Is that right? Kill me? Just like you killed your parents? Jamie told me about the newspaper clippings. It didn't take a rocket scientist to figure that one out."

Teri became enraged with silent anger.

Jim reached into his denim jacket and pulled a small kitchen knife he had stolen that morning and pointed it at her. "You don't scare me! Where's the others?" he yelled.

Teri reared back the large, steel axe, "Don't worry Jim, you will all be together soon," she cried out as she brought the axe down in a swinging motion severing Jim's arm. Jim, in a state of shock, stumbled backwards as Teri continued her violent assault on him. She continued until he was barely recognizable.

After the anger wore off Tina was hungry and tired. She decided to head back in the direction of the cabin in hopes of finding Jim on the way. She was no longer pissed at him. So she decided to walk back to the nearby creek to see if Jim was still there. When Tina found her way to where she had left Jim she saw the gruesome remains, though it took her a few minutes to realize that it was Jim. At that moment she let out an earsplitting scream. She stumbled backwards, trying to get away from the bloody remains that was once her boyfriend. Tina finally got her footing and turned to run but stopped short in her tracks when Teri appeared in front of her covered in blood and still clutching the bloody axe. "Oh my God, Teri. You killed Jim!" she screamed between sobs.

"Don't worry Tina, you deserved better," Teri quietly said.
Tina turned to run, Teri lifted the heavy axe and swiftly chopped her head off; it tumbled down the bank and into the nearby creek.

THE GATHERING

Jamie and Paul desperately tried to make their way back to the cabin as midnight approached. Paul was overwhelmed with pain.

"Jamie, Jamie hold up," he cried. "My arm Jamie, I can't...the pain."

Jamie knew that Paul couldn't make it one more step so she eased him down on a nearby stump to rest. She told him that as soon as she returned from the cabin, regardless if she found the others or not, then they would leave.

"Okay. I will just wait here but I'm letting you go under protest. Be careful and hurry back," he told her.

"I'll be back as soon as I can," she replied.

Jamie quickly made her way back to the cabin. She slowly opened the door. She quietly entered the living room of the dark cabin. The fire, once alive and blazing, was nearly dead. She saw Doug's smart phone lying on the hearth. Jamie began to search the old cabin, looking for her friends or for clues to that would lead her to them. Jamie finally made her way to Teri's bedroom. When she reached down and tried to turn the knob she found the door was locked. Jamie went back into the living room and noticed something she hadn't seen earlier—an old book bound in black leather placed beside a large crystal orb on the rosewood coffee table. Jamie slowly bent down and opened the large, dusty, mysterious text. Soon enough Jamie discovered it wasn't just an old book, but rather, a Witches book of human sacrifice.

"Oh my God! The sheriff was right...Teri Black is a Witch!" A horrified Jamie bumped the book and knocked it to the floor. Just then, a small object flew out, and across the floor. To her surprise a skeleton key flew out of the book when it hit the floor. She stooped over and picked it up. "Oh my God! I bet this is the key to the bedroom," Jamie thought aloud. The name 'Daniel' had been inscribed on it. Jamie now wondered why that name was inscribed on it...regardless, she thought she may now have access to the locked bedroom. Despite her better judgment, Jamie decided to go back to the bedroom and try the key. She hoped that it would give her access to the bedroom. She tried the key and it worked. As she opened the bedroom door the strange fragrance of incense and wax perforated the room, and a warm glowing light illuminated the room with dim orange.

Jamie let out a blood curling scream as she found her what was left of her three friends on Teri's bed. The overwhelming scent of blood and the remains of dozens of lit candles cut a deeply disturbing and macabre image in Jamie's mind. "Doug! Tina! Jim!" she cried out in shock. She quickly slammed the door closed and frantically ran out of the cabin.

Jamie ran out onto the porch and was amazed to see Paul there. "Paul! Paul! Get up! We need to leave!" she screamed. She reached down to try to help him up only to discover he was also dead. Jamie screamed uncontrollably. She cried over Paul's body.

Teri Black appeared from the darkness, axe in hand and walked toward the porch. Jamie was frozen in fear as Teri approached. Teri, her axe covered in the blood of her friends, smiled as she closed in on Jamie.

"You killed Paul!" Jamie screamed.

"I did," Teri coldly responded, ice in her eyes. Teri now outstretched her arm toward Jamie. "Come with me, Jamie," she said. Jamie, shocked and confused turned to run but tripped and fell. She hit head hard on a woodened support post holding up the roof of the porch. She was knocked unconscious.

THE SACRIFICE

It was November. The moon, once high in the night sky was now beginning to lower. Halloween was over; however, its darkness and evil still had several hours to live.

Jamie McLaughlin, the last member of the group, found herself lying on a large ominous sacrificial stone alter in the middle of a clearing in the forest. Her arms and legs were strapped down by old, dried leather straps bolted to the altar. The straps were firm and tight around her hands and feet. Now awake and aware of her surroundings, Jamie lye there gazing up into the starry heavens. The stars above her formed a unique constellation; the constellation was in the shape of a side-triangle, the runic symbol of future vision and message, also known as the symbol of Thorn, which Teri carried on her body.

Struggling to free herself from the tight bonds of the straps, Jamie began to look around the clearing for an escape route. Jamie's stomach sank as she noticed the five stones with strange symbols carved in them that surrounded her.

Teri appeared from the darkness. "Well, you're finally awake." Teri noticed that Jamie was looking at the stones. "Oh, would you like to know what these symbols mean? Well, they are all bearing the Wiccan symbols of Earth, Air, Fire, Water and Spirit. They aren't randomly laid; they form a gigantic pentagram—a direct gateway to the constellation, now almost directly overhead and you are in the very center of it all."

Teri Black, the master mind and gatekeeper, had a grand plan. "Now, the real game begins" she said as she pulled a long, sharp, Celtic dagger from her sash."

Jamie, fully aware of Teri's intentions, desperately struggled to free herself. "Why are you doing this Teri?" she asked.

Teri replied, "Unlike those looser friends of yours, I truly like you and hate to sacrifice you. Alas I have no other choice."

"Teri, you don't have to sacrifice me—you don't—you really don't. It's never too late to do the right thing," Jamie pleaded. Just then Jamie saw remorse in Teri's eyes.

Teri's piercing green eyes now lowered and her hand clinching the long ceremonial dagger lowered to her side. She began to explain her motives. "The past 31 years—the past 31 Halloweens—I have needed a pure and true virgin to sacrifice. However, my offerings were never good enough—none were ever truly pure. It's different now Jamie, this will be the season to end all seasons—the true final harvest. The gods have brought you to me and it's time to deliver you to them. I will now gain what's rightfully mine…all the knowledge of the future!"

Just then, a surge of evil anger raged across Teri's face and any trace of tender humanity vanished from her soul. Teri quickly stepped forward and raised the ceremonial dagger to stab Jamie.

Without warning a large, ear-splitting bang pierced the night air, stunning Teri.

"Freeze! Put it down!" echoed a deep but familiar voice. "I don't think you want to know your future."

Teri and Jamie both looked in the direction of the voice and were surprised to see an unexpected sight…Sherriff Ron Thomas was alive. He was obviously seriously injured but alive no less. The sheriff stood there holding a large Colt .357 magnum python revolver in his hand.

"It's over Karen. Let the girl go," he commanded. "I won't let you kill one more person," he told Teri as he pulled the hammer back into position for another shot. Jamie's struggling had finally paid off. She pulled hard against one of the straps on her hand and it broke. A distracted Teri advanced on the sheriff with dagger in hand.

"I know why you did it. I know why you killed your parents," the sheriff told her. "I know about Daniel, your boyfriend."

At the sound of Daniel's name, Teri's eyes lowered and she became very pale. Obviously a nerve had been struck. Teri began to tell a story. "It was February 1981and I was sixteen at the time. My parents were strict—Episcopal deacons at our local church… everything I did…every move I made was governed by them. I hated them for that. Then there was a boy—this one boy who arrived in our community. His name was Daniel. He wasn't your average seventeen-year-old; he was shy and very thoughtful. He had autism and had no friends. Soon, it was obvious that he liked me, and I liked him too. One day something bad happened— something truly evil. Daniel walked to our house to ask me out to the upcoming Valentine's Day event at our church. My parents told Daniel that I didn't like him, and that he was overstepping his bounds for arriving at our home. He turned and ran away. Later that day news of his death spread like wildfire. Devastated he laid down on a railroad track that day," she concluded.

"So you killed your parents for what they did, and then you became a witch to get back at the Religion that caused it," the sheriff responded as he lowered his gun and reached for his hand cuffs. Jamie completely free now grabbed a large stone lying on the ground.

A sadistic grin crept across Teri's face, "I guess so; they deserved it… and now it's your turn!" she cried out in a demonic voice. Teri Black, entirely overcome with evil, cast a spell over the Sherriff forcing him to raise his revolver to his mouth. Powerless to stop himself he pulled the trigger. Jamie lunged at Teri with the bolder held high above her head and hit Teri hard on the back of the head. Teri went down to her knees dazed and confused dropping the dagger. Jamie took this opportunity to seize the dagger and stabbed Teri through the heart. Teri died almost instantly.

ONE YEAR LATER

In the rural, ominous foothills of Hampshire County, West Virginia Halloween Eve as leaves began to fall the sun began to set. A small grey sedan pulled into a clearing deep in the woods. Not far away, in a wooded glade, was a small log cabin. A young, newly wedded couple stepped out of the car. "There it is. It's perfect for a honeymoon!" the man told his new wife. The young wife now glanced over to see an owl perched in a nearby tree watching them.

"Are you sure this is our cabin?" she asked as a strange sense of dread came over her. "Maybe we should find another cabin," she said nervously. "Honey, I promise you, the woman who owns it gave us a great deal. Please, just give it a chance," he asked of her as he kissed her cheek. They walked up to the cabin, never imagining the grisly horror that was to ensue in the next few moments—never to know the evil truth…of Witch Cabin.

The End.

ABOUT THE AUTHOR

Born on July 29th, 1988 in Hattiesburg, Mississippi. Jake Galjour isn't your average southerner . From an early age, Jakes fascination with horror films and the supernatural have brought him both friendship and misfortune with his fellow southern community. Raised primarily by his mother, Cynthia, he eventually received a general education diploma in 2012. His interest include horror movies, new wave music and Halloween.

www.ingramcontent.com/pod-product-compliance
Lightning Source LLC
Chambersburg PA
CBHW020612130626

46552CB00007B/3169